Dedicated to the children who live in the Canadian Boreal Forest, especially those who acted as my consultants for this book. I hope this book answers most of your questions about the fox.

The author gratefully acknowledges the helpful comments and suggestions provided by J. David Henry, Ph.D.

Note for Librarians: A cataloguing record for this book is available from Library and Archives
Canada at www.collectionscanada.ca/amicus/index-e.html
ISBN 1-4120-8241-2

*Printed in Victoria, BC, Canada. Printed on paper with minimum 30% recycled fibre. Trafford's print shop
runs on "green energy" from solar, wind and other environmentally-friendly power sources.*

TRAFFORD
PUBLISHING™

Offices in Canada, USA, Ireland and UK

This book was published *on-demand* in cooperation with Trafford Publishing. On-demand
publishing is a unique process and service of making a book available for retail sale to the
public taking advantage of on-demand manufacturing and Internet marketing. On-demand
publishing includes promotions, retail sales, manufacturing, order fulfilment, accounting and
collecting royalties on behalf of the author.

Book sales for North America and international:
Trafford Publishing, 6E–2333 Government St.,
Victoria, BC V8T 4P4 CANADA
phone 250 383 6864 (toll-free 1 888 232 4444)
fax 250 383 6804; email to orders@trafford.com
Book sales in Europe:
Trafford Publishing (UK) Limited, 9 Park End Street, 2nd Floor
Oxford, UK OX1 1HH UNITED KINGDOM
phone 44 (0)1865 722 113 (local rate 0845 230 9601)
facsimile 44 (0)1865 722 868; info.uk@trafford.com
Order online at:
trafford.com/05-3207

10 9 8 7 6 5 4 3 2

I am a fox. I belong to the dog family.

I am covered with long, soft fur. This makes me look much larger than I really am.

It is easy to recognize me. I am an attractive and wise looking animal. My ears are pointed and my white-tipped tail is long and bushy. However, some red foxes do not have a white tip on their tail, but they are perfectly healthy! Foxhunters call my tail a brush.

My father — as are all male foxes — is called a dog fox. My mother — as are all female foxes — is called a vixen. Surprisingly, baby foxes can be called cubs, pups, or kits.

My father is about one hundred fifteen cm from the tip of his nose to the tip of his tail. He stands about thirty cm at the shoulder and weighs five kg. This is how big I expect to be when I grow up.

My mother is smaller and weighs less than my father.

My father and mother want a nice, warm den for their newborn litter. They begin by looking for a deserted den or burrow. They clean it out, and make it the size they need. They also add more entrances. If they cannot find a deserted den, then they will dig a new one in loose sandy soil.

Actually, my parents will have an extra den or two ready in case of an emergency. My parents are cunning and canny when it comes to protecting their young!

My mother has a litter of pups numbering from two to eight during the early spring. When snowshoe hares are rare, she may not have a litter that year. I am very tiny and helpless when I am born. I weigh only one hundred twenty grams and I am about fifteen cm long.

At birth, my brothers and sisters are covered with fuzzy grayish brown fur. We are born blind, toothless and without hearing. When we are small, it's also freezing down in our secure den. This is why my mother never leaves us alone for the first ten days of our lives. We need her for warmth as well as for our milk, which she feeds us!

While my mother looks after us, my father hunts for food. After he catches it, he brings it to the entrance of the den and leaves it there for her. She does not trust my father to be with us and she alone is in the den with us during this time. She needs much food because she breast-feeds all of us.

My eyes open when I am ten days old, and our coats are warmer. Now, my mother can leave us alone while she goes hunting for her own food. She loves us too much to go very far. She looks for food close to the den, always taking care that we are safe. If she hears or sees danger approaching, she gives a loud alarm call, and we go to sleep, deep down in the den. Later, she will return to the den and may carry us one by one, in her mouth to another den.

When I am a month old, I begin to be very curious about the world outside
the den. Together with my brothers and sisters, I leave the safety of the
den. At first, we are very afraid of all sounds. The soft song of a bird,
the screech of an owl, and the bark of a dog are all new and frightening
noises. Until we learn which are really friendly, and which are not, we
hide from all noises.

The hoot of an owl is one noise that my mother teaches us to listen to and hide from as soon as we hear it. The great gray owl (the largest of all owls) is one enemy that loves pups for her meal! It sits on a high perch and has a good view of all that moves below. One swift swoop and I could be just a delightful memory!

Soon, I, together with my brothers and sisters, lose this great fear. We begin to play near the entrance of the den. We wrestle, tumble, chase and play tag. We also fight. That helps determine who gets the food that our parents bring to the den. I am a powerful pup!

Even before leaving the safety of the den, we begin eating meat. Both our parents come into the den with small animals or larger animals cut into small pieces for us to eat.

We stay together all summer, playing and learning many new things. In the fall most of us go our separate ways. Though they stay in the family territory even my father and mother each go in their own direction, until February, when they will meet and begin a new family. Sometimes one of my sisters will stay with my parents and help raise the litter born next spring. I will be ready to begin my own family in February.

Strange as it may seem — not all my brothers and sisters will grow "red" fur when they lose their baby fur. Though we have the same parents, some of my brothers and sisters could be silver, some black and some cross. The cross fox is yellowish or reddish brown with a black or dark brown band of fur that runs across the neck from shoulder to shoulder and another band that goes down the back. Most of us that are "red" are also different shades of red. Shades of brown, golden-brown, bronze or rust are all common.

My coat is made up of two kinds of fur. A short, thick wooly undercoat and long stiff guard hairs. It is the color of the guard hairs that gives me my color.

However, my fur is darkest on my back and behind my head. My chin, chest, under parts, and insides of my back legs are white. The fur on the back of my ears is blackish.

My legs are adapted for running. My favorite way of getting from place to place is by trotting. I can trot seven kilometers an hour without getting exhausted. When running away from an enemy I can run about seventy kilometers an hour. Very few enemies can catch me!

Remember my white-tipped tail also called the brush? It is between twenty-five and thirty-five centimeters long. I use it as a balancing pole or as a rudder when I make sharp turns very quickly or when I am speeding down slopes.

The winters are very cold and the snow is deep in the forests where I live. A thick tuft of stiff hair grows between my toe pads. This tuft of hair does two things for me. First it gives me a better grip on slippery places, like snow and ice. Then, it also keeps my feet warm. If snow collects on this tuft of hair, then freezes into a ball, I can take it off with my warm tongue and teeth.

In winter, when I sleep in the snow, I curl into a tight ball and fold my tail over my feet and nose. My tail becomes my blanket and keeps me warm.

My hearing is very keen! I can hear the squeak of mice from quite a distance and can pinpoint them when they scurry underneath the snow. However, my sense of smell is sharper still. If the wind is blowing towards me, I can smell the scent of man or any meat that he puts out for me, even from a few kilometers away. My eyesight is also very keen and I depend on it for getting my food.

My favorite food is the vole, then the field mouse. I also eat frogs but never toads. I like different kinds of food. I eat rabbits, squirrels, birds, bird eggs, berries and grass. In the summer and fall, beetles, crickets, and grasshoppers are a nice change of diet. I even enjoy an occasional fish. A special treat is the larvae of wasps!! Oh, yes, I have had a few stings — but not enough to chase me away forever. When I am hungry and cannot find fresh food, I eat the meat leftover after the bears and wolves have had their fill.

My teeth are very special. Let me tell you about them. My teeth stay sharp and hard because a new coat of enamel grows each year! You can even find out how old I am by counting the enamel rings on my teeth!

Remember that I belong to the dog family? So just like dogs, foxes talk to each other in many different ways. We bark, cry, yelp, whine, howl, and even squeal and scream. I learned when I was very young that a low growl means "DANGER. QUICK HIDE."

My enemies, or predators, are the coyote, wolf, lynx and the biggest of all is MAN. If I can keep away from these predators, I can live to be at least twelve years old. That is old age for a fox.

Also by Olga Majola
I AM A MOOSE Let Me Tell You About Myself

Olga Majola

Linch Curry

Olga Majola holds a B.A., B. Ed., and a M. Ed. She has spent 25 years teaching elementary school, with 4 of those years being spent in fly-in communities located in the Canadian Boreal Forest. She and her husband have spent the past 9 years living and working in Pelly Crossing, Yukon. This is Olga's second book and she is currently at work on her third.

Linch Curry is very well known in the Yukon as an artist, teacher, trapper, fisher and hunter. She is a respected elder of the Selkirk First Nation of Pelly Crossing, Yukon, where she resides with her husband. Linch's unique style of artwork reflects her deep understanding and her love of the land that she was born on.

Olga Majola
Learning & Growth Centre
Box 51
Pelly Crossing, Yukon Y0B 1P0
Tel: (867) 537-3925   Fax: (867) 537-3501
Email: omajola2002@yahoo.ca